LITTLE MOUSE ON THE PRAIRIE

Written By:
STEPHEN COSGROVE

Illustrated By:
ROBIN JAMES

GROLIER ENTERPRISES INC.
Danbury, Connecticut

A Serendipity Book

Grolier Enterprises, Inc. offers a varied selection of
both adult and children's book racks. For details on
ordering, please write: Grolier Enterprises, Inc.,
Sherman Turnpike, Danbury, CT 06816 Attn:
Premium Department

FGHIJK R 987654

Dedicated to Robert James, a dedicated man who taught me the lessons learned by Tweezle.
Stephen

In a land of dew drops and day dreams, near absolutely nothing at all, lived a whole bunch of mice.

Now, these mice weren't your average run-of-the-mill house-mouse mice. They were more like meadow mice that you might mingle with on a medium morning in May or maybe March.

From dawn to dusk through spring and early summer, they would skitter and scurry across the prairie without a single care in the world.

They would race about and then suddenly leap high in the air to touch the wings of a golden butterfly or sometimes they would do nothing at all except sniff the flowers.

All the mice of the prairie were like this, except for one small mouse called Tweezle Dee. While the other mice were playing their silly games, Tweezle Dee or, as the other mice called her, Tweeze, would work industriously, doing all sorts of tedious chores.

As soon as she woke in the morning, right after eating her breakfast and brushing her teeth, she would begin a long day of hard work.

She would dash this way and that, collecting twigs, branches and brambles with which to build her new winter home.

Tweeze worked for months and months as the other mice played in the meadow. If she wasn't working on her house she would be off and about collecting nuts and berries and storing them away for the winter. She never stopped to play but was always on the go, searching for this or that and working, working, working.

The only things she never did were smile or laugh. Tweeze thought that smiling and laughing was a waste of time, and she barely had enough time to do her chores as it was.

The other mice of the meadow would stop their play just to watch Tweeze work. They would laugh 'til they could laugh no more, watching her dash from place to place searching for the perfect leaf or a just so twig.

Sometimes it was great fun for the other mice to see if they could get Tweeze to smile. As she would race by they would jump in front of her making faces that should have made a statue smile. She would always just shrug her shoulders and say, "Silly mouse! I have no time to smile. For winter is coming and I have work to do!" Then she would move quickly on her grumbly way.

One day the mice ran out of fun things to do. They sat in the meadow and thought and thought, hoping to find some new game to play.

"I know what we can do!" said one of the mice brightly. "Let's play a joke on that old grouch mouse, Tweezle Dee." He hurriedly whispered his plan to the other mice.

They all giggled in delight and set off in a million directions to gather what they needed for their wonderful joke. From every flower in the meadow they picked all the pollen that their little arms could hold. Then, they carefully placed the pollen high in the branches of a tree that spread over the path that she took every day to and from the meadow. When everything was in its place the mice hid at the base of the tree, giggling as they waited for Tweezle Dee.

Sure enough, not a moment or two later, Tweeze came trudging along the trail.

One of the mice, as usual, jumped in front of her and made a ridiculously funny face.

"Out of my way, silly mouse!" she said. "I have work to do, for winter is on its way."

"No. Winter has already come," said the little mouse as he tried to hide a smile.

Tweeze looked about the meadow and said solemnly, "No it hasn't. Look around, mouse. There is no snow."

With that the other mice shook the tree, causing the pollen to fall on top of poor Tweezle Dee like snowfall in deep December. They all laughed and laughed but she just glared and said, "Mark my words, winter is coming and when it does you silly mice won't be laughing so hard!"

"Old grouch!" they chanted as she moved on her way. "She doesn't know what she's talking about." Then they began rolling and playing in the pollen.

Sure enough, just as she had predicted, winter did come to the meadow. In a swoosh of clouds, wind and snow, the whole meadow was crystal white and quite still.

At first the mice found the snow to be just another game, but as the day wore on it became colder and colder.

"What are we to do!" cried the mice through chattering teeth. "Tweeze was right, we should have worked to prepare for winter. Now we shall surely freeze."

They all huddled together and one of them said, "We must go to Tweeze, maybe she can help."

All the meadow mice made their way through the falling snow to Tweeze's house on the far side of the meadow. They gathered about and softly tapped on the door.

"Who is it?" came the reply.

"It is mice of the meadow," they answered.

The door opened slowly and there stood Tweeze all warm and cozy in a sweater she had knitted the summer before. Behind her the other mice could see a warm, crackling fire made of twigs she had gathered in the fall. "What do you want?" growled Tweeze. "Have you come to play another silly joke on me?"

"No," said one of the mice. "We came to say we were sorry for all the things we did, and that you were right—winter was coming and we should have prepared ourselves as you did." Then all the mice cried, "Please, Tweeze, can't we stay with you? If you refuse we shall surely freeze!"

Tweeze shrugged her shoulders and said, "You should have thought of that before!" And with that she closed the door.

Tweeze busied herself, stoking the fire and cleaning house. But you know what? Never in her life had she ever smiled, nor had she been happy. In fact, she was very, very lonely.

She tried to keep busy, but day after day all she could think about was those poor freezing mice somewhere out in the snow-covered meadow.

Finally she could stand it no more, and after putting on her winter coat and mittens, she set out to find the mice. For you see Tweeze had a plan—a very happy plan.

After searching for many hours, she finally found them huddled in a snow bank beneath a scraggly bush.

With a frozen tear in her eye, she told them her plan.

"Fellow mice," she began, "through the summer I worked as you played, preparing for winter. Many times I wanted to join you but I didn't know how. If you will teach me how to have fun, I will teach you how to spin and weave and I will share my home with you."

The mice quickly agreed and they all set off for the warmth of Tweeze's home.

What a merry time they had. Tweeze taught them to weave, and sew, and they taught her to laugh and sing.

And once or twice, for no reason at all, Tweezle Dee would smile a happy smile.

So, when you're hard at work or working hard at play, remember Tweezle's laughter on that crystal winter's day.